DISNEP
PIRATES of the C...
JACK SPARROW

Sins of the Father

by Rob Kidd
Illustrated by Jean-Paul Orpinas

Based on the earlier life of the character, Jack Sparrow,
created for the theatrical motion picture,
"Pirates of the Caribbean: The Curse of the Black Pearl"
Screen Story by Ted Elliott & Terry Rossio and Stuart Beattie and Jay Wolpert,
Screenplay by Ted Elliott & Terry Rossio,
and characters created for the theatrical motion pictures
"Pirates of the Caribbean: Dead Man's Chest" and
"Pirates of the Caribbean: At World's End"
written by Ted Elliott & Terry Rossio

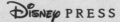

DISNEP PRESS

New York

Special thanks to
Rich Thomas and Ken Becker

First Edition
1 3 5 7 9 10 8 6 4 2

Library of Congress Catalog Card Number: 2007904363

ISBN-13: 978-1-4231-0455-1
ISBN-10: 1-4231-0455-2

DISNEYPIRATES.COM

Sins of the Father

CHAPTER ONE

*I*magine for a moment that you are a runaway, fleeing from a way of life you are not sure you want, but fear you might be destined for. Your household is full of pirates who terrorize the Seven Seas . . . and each other. Family reunions, holiday celebrations, and strolls in the park inevitably crumble into massive brawls where the kids are suddenly beating up their uncle, Captain "Ace" Brannigan. Then, second-auntie "Quick Draw" McFleming tosses yet another tankard at poor old Grandmama (who even at eighty-two is not so defenseless, what with the half-dozen daggers she keeps tucked away in her girdle). While all this is going on, the man who's been raising you—who may or may not be your father—is plotting some way to overthrow the current patriarch and secure the family inheritance of plundered treasure for himself.

You might, in circumstances like these, decide that you need some time away . . . to leave the madness behind for a while and set aside a few days, or weeks, or perhaps even years, to think things through.

So, to get things started, one night, after the family's had a particularly rough day and everyone is knocked out (either from exhaustion or from having been throttled over the head with a blunt object), you strike a match and sneak by candlelight into the study. It's a room housing a three-legged chair, a handful of dusty old books with some pages missing, and dozens upon dozens of half-empty rum bottles. Apart from the thick cover of cobwebs and an occasional tarantula, the only other item in the room is a huge leather-bound book, the size of a tombstone, marked PIRATA CODEX. You know that this book is important to your family and, in fact, to all pirates. It is the law that they live by, and you are going to use it to your advantage.

You turn to a section that is all about freedom and the need for a pirate to make decisions for himself. You decide that this clearly gives you justification to leave this maddening household with these intolerable people you call your family. With a wry smile, you close the heavy cover. Then you make your way over to the far end of the room, pry the nails out of the window, which, like the others in the house, has been boarded up for as long as you have lived there. And suddenly, you are free. It's as easy as that.

Or is it?

For the young man called Jack Sparrow, nothing about this scenario is hypothetical. As unbelievable as it might be, this is his life story, or at least part of it. Shortly after Jack snuck away, he realized that his newfound freedom had come at a heavy price.

Maybe The-Man-Who-Might-Be-Dad hadn't always supported him in his hobbies (he'd had, for example, a particularly difficult time understanding Jack's interest in cosmetics), but he *had* been there to knock Rusty Knickers over the head just before the pirate nearly severed Jack's hand with his crusty old sword when Jack was six. And when Captain Lucille Graven attempted to sell

Jack into servitude at the age of twelve, The-Man-Who-Might-Be-Dad was there again, ready to save Jack's hide. But now, Jack was suddenly going about everything on his own. And, though he didn't want to admit it, part of him was not sure he was ready for that kind of freedom.

He *did* know that he did not want to be like the rest of the family. He didn't want to be a pirate. He did, however, want to be a captain, just like The-Man-Who-Might-Be-Dad, whose name was Teague. Whenever he was aboard Teague's ship, Jack thought to himself, Now how hard can this be? You just assemble any group of seafaring dolts . . . apparently half of which can be drunk at any given time . . . hop on a ship, give yourself the proper air of authority that makes said dolts adhere to your whims as you bark orders, and voilà!

So, one of the first things Jack did upon securing his freedom was find a boat. It was called the *Barnacle*, and it was a rickety old vessel that was barely seaworthy. Then he assembled a crew. But since that time, things had changed. Though he still had his boat, his crew had abandoned him. All of his crew, that is, with the exception of one crewmember—Fitzwilliam P. Dalton III.

From the outset, Jack did not like Fitzwilliam, and he certainly hadn't wanted him to join his crew. But the boy, who claimed to have been a runaway aristocrat, put Jack in a very compromising position. Fitzwilliam had threatened to turn Jack in for the theft of the *Barnacle* if he did not allow Fitzwilliam to come aboard. When Jack still refused, Fitzwilliam challenged him to a duel. Jack hadn't been trained in swordsmanship the way Fitzwilliam had. Though Jack put up a valiant fight, Fitzwilliam overcame him, and the rest, as they say, is history.

For about a year now, the two had been sailing together. Jack had to admit that there was some value in having Fitzwilliam on board. He was an excellent swordsman, and whenever Jack's ragged crew needed to blend in with "proper" society, Fitzwilliam was a helpful cover. Still, Jack and Fitzwilliam were often bickering and never quite saw eye-to-eye on matters of navigating the *Barnacle* or responding to threats from pirates, sea creatures, and cursed captains. In truth—not that he would have dared admit it—something deep inside Jack actually enjoyed the bitter back-and-forth. He loved antagonizing Fitzwilliam, and there was nothing Jack savored more than working the aristocrat into an apoplectic fit of rage. But it always seemed that that was where their rivalry ended. Until now.

Because now, Jack found himself on the deck of the *Barnacle*, holding up his hands, with Fitzwilliam's sword pointed at his chest. Even Jack, who prided himself on having a type of sixth sense, had not seen this coming.

"You were a fool to trust me," Fitzwilliam said. He wore a half-insane grin.

"Who ever said I trusted you, mate? I trust no one," Jack said sincerely.

"Why else would you have kept me aboard your vessel, 'Captain'?"

"Because I had a need, and you were able to fill it. Savvy?" Jack replied curtly.

The aristocrat sneered. "You make me ill at ease," he snarled.

"Then I am doing a right fine job!" Jack said, inching away from Fitzwilliam.

Jack had been so taken aback by this turn

of events that he had almost forgotten that Fitzwilliam was only *one* of the problems plaguing him at this very moment.

Jack turned and looked out to sea, and what seemed to be the entire Royal Navy, along with some East India Trading Company ships, were fast approaching the *Barnacle*. Perhaps worse than this was the vessel that the fleet was pursuing. It was a pirate ship, and it flew a Jolly Roger that Jack was all too familiar with. He regarded each of these three threats, which formed a deadly triangle around him.

Before him was an aristocrat who Jack hadn't necessarily trusted, but who he also never suspected of being capable of this kind of treachery. And yet, here he was, holding Jack at bay, while a fleet of navy ships brought up the rear.

And the navy ships were, of course,

another problem to consider. Fitzwilliam had alluded to the fact that he was working with them. That their goal was to use Jack to lead them to Teague. This would not make Teague happy.

Which led Jack to problem number three—that ship with the familiar Jolly Roger trying to flee the navy belonged to the pirate that might be Jack's dad. And, father or not, Teague was not very pretty when he was angry.

Jack sighed in frustration. These three bitter ingredients were surely a recipe for disaster.

CHAPTER TWO

"Look here," Jack said to Fitzwilliam, when he had fully digested the various terrible scenarios before him. "You can't mutiny. Besides not being very democratic, it would make you rather *stupid*."

"You *dare* saddle me with that epithet? *You*, who allowed me to come aboard your ship and trail you until you led me to the notorious Captain Teague? Please Jack, let us be reasonable and fair. *You* are the stupid one among us," Fitzwilliam spat back.

"Well, stupid's relative, ain't it, Fitzy? See, here you are thinking I am the one lacking the smarts, while I would say that it is you, who voluntarily picked a fight with Teague over there. Trust me, I've been there. You're not going to win."

"Perhaps you forget that I have brought reinforcements," Fitzwilliam said smugly, motioning to the Royal Navy ships that were still on course for the *Barnacle*.

"Teague's evaded them before," Jack said, stretching and yawning. "This will just be further practice for him. See, in the end, you're helping him out. But, here we are digressing, when we should be continuing our argument or some such. So, getting back to the subject . . ."

"Yes," Fitzwilliam said, "getting back to the subject . . . prepare to meet your fate." Fitzwilliam quickly drew his shiny sword.

"Actually, Fitzy, the subject at hand was not swordplay, but stupidity, and you are proving your own strength in that department by forgetting that it was the topic under discussion." Jack now drew his old, rusty sword with the golden tip. "And, if you remember, though you probably don't, as a lamebrain like you can barely seem to remember that the Florida coast is west of the Antilles, what I was referring to as 'stupid' was your plot to mutiny. And, just because you didn't ask, and because there is nothing I love more than boring people—quite especially you—with details, I posit that it's a stupid idea because it takes a crew to mutiny. A *crew*, mate. Not one well-dressed, stuffy aristocrat who doesn't even have enough mental agility to figure out how to use contractions when he's speaking."

Fitzwilliam's face went red. "Ah, were you an *actual* captain, aboard an *actual* ship, I might agree with you. However, you're nothing other than a small, insignificant boy aboard a ship that's always two minutes away from taking on water and capsizing."

Jack sneered at Fitzwilliam, then looked around, casually glancing at the *Barnacle* and the ragged state it was in, before resigning to these facts and shrugging in agreement.

"Now, 'Captain'," Fitzwilliam went on, pointing his sword at Jack's belly. "Please vacate this ship. It is the property of the East India Trading Company."

"Over my dead body," Jack said casually, examining the dirt beneath his fingernails.

"If that is what you wish . . ." Fitzwilliam said, crashing his sword down toward Jack's head. Jack lifted his own sword, defending himself against the heavy blow. The telltale clank of metal against metal heralded the beginning of their fight. The clanging rang out as they continued to spar, providing a musical score for their deadly dance.

"Recognize these here moves of mine, Fitzy?" Jack asked.

Fitzwilliam just snarled.

"Well, you should. Who do you think I learned them from?" Jack said as he nimbly jumped onto the *Barnacle*'s railing and moved across it in a crablike fashion as the boys continued to spar.

Jack's sword-fighting abilities were, in fact, very similar to Fitzwilliam's. Jack had been watching the other boy and examining his moves for the past year, and he had learned much. One thing Jack Sparrow knew was that in order to get the upper hand, one had to acknowledge his own deficits and work hard, however subtly, to overcome them. Jack had never been a very good sword-fighter. Fitzwilliam, on the other hand, though Jack hated to admit it, was an expert. So Jack had watched and learned, and though even he himself might not have known it, Jack was becoming an expert, too.

"Jackie!" a voice called out behind Jack. "Where on earth did you learn to fight like that? You were always so—well, frankly, awful!"

Jack spun around, turning his eyes from his opponent and toward the man's voice that boomed behind him, all the while still successfully deflecting Fitzwilliam's attack.

"Oh, it's you," Jack said flatly.

Teague's ship had caught up with the *Barnacle*. The pirate was standing at the broadside, smiling down at Jack. He was a tall man with ragged, curly hair and a bandana similar to Jack's tied around his head. His long red overcoat looked like a cape, and he wore a sword on each of his hips. Every one of his fingers was adorned with a ring.

Jack hated Teague's casual demeanor. He had such a disgusting air of confidence. What looked like the entire Royal Navy was on Teague's tail, and yet here he stood, looking down at Jack battling away, with an insouciance that indicated absolutely no worry whatsoever.

Teague's mannerisms just confirmed what Jack already knew. Teague wasn't worried in the least. Davy Jones, the cursed captain who sailed the ghost ship the *Flying Dutchman* and was feared all over the Seven Seas, could have emerged in front of them right now, complicating this already impossible situation further, and Teague would not bat an eye. It was stomach-turning.

"You think you might want to help me out here?" Jack asked, still deflecting Fitzwilliam's blows. Fitzwilliam seemed to be so focused on defeating his opponent that the aristocrat didn't even acknowledge the appearance of Teague, or the banter between him and Jack. Jack thought that Fitzwilliam's silence spoke volumes about how intent he was on killing Jack. The snotty aristocrat usually couldn't keep his mouth shut.

"You didn't seem to want any help when you decided to run out on us, Jackie," Teague responded.

"I don't need this right now," Jack said.

"Dear old Grandmama nearly died of grief when you left," Teague said.

"Dear old Grandmama has tried to *kill* me on three separate occasions," Jack said.

"That was her way of showing you she *loved* you, Jackie," Teague replied.

"Ughh!" Jack yelled in frustration. Jack again turned his back on Teague and focused the anger that was welling up within him on Fitzwilliam. Their swords clashed louder, and Jack suddenly became as determined to win the fight as Fitzwilliam.

"Why can't anyone . . ." Jack yelled at the top of his lungs, "just leave me . . ." His face grew redder and redder. "*Alone!*"

Fitzwilliam's eyes grew wide, and if Jack could have seen Teague's he would have noticed them popping as well. Neither of them had ever seen Jack act like this before. He was usually so calm and cool and collected. It was clear that he was having a little bit of an anger-management issue here. His reaction took Fitzwilliam so off guard that the aristocrat tripped on some loose lines on the deck, falling against the *Barnacle*'s port side. He was now at Jack's mercy.

"Jack," Fitzwilliam said, holding up his hands. It wasn't clear what type of an appeal he was going to make. Would he apologize? Gloss this whole mutiny thing over somehow? Jack didn't care.

"Don't dare say another word," Jack said. "Get up."

Fitzwilliam shuffled to his feet. He was still attempting to maintain his strong, proud demeanor, but it was clear his near defeat was worrying him.

"Get off my boat," Jack said, pointing his sword at Fitzwilliam's neck and breathing heavily with anger.

"Now, Jack . . ."

"I don't care where you go after you're off, but get off. Swim to the 'royal pains' back there, swim to the East India Trading Company slave ships, swim over to Teague and sail off into the sunset together. I don't care where the devil you go. Just go. Now," Jack said.

Fitzwilliam stood stock-still.

"*Now!*" Jack yelled, raising his sword and bringing it down swiftly before Fitzwilliam. This caused the aristocrat to stumble, and as he lost his balance, Jack quickly pushed him overboard using the handle of his sword. There was a dull splash. Jack didn't look overboard. He didn't want to. He sunk down onto the deck, hugged his legs and buried his face in his knees.

"Nice job, Jackie!" came Teague's voice from the adjoining ship.

"Oh, shut up," Jack said flatly.

CHAPTER THREE

$\mathcal{J}$ack sat there on the *Barnacle*'s deck for
what felt like a long while, but in truth it
was at most a few short minutes. He sat
there thinking about his options. The navy
wasn't really after *him*, were they? Fitzwilliam
had said it himself. They just wanted to use
Jack in order to find Teague. It was the
Keeper of the Code they wanted, not Jack.
So why was Jack so worried?

He was worried because, despite running
away from home, assembling a crew, and

experiencing adventures upon the high seas, there was still one thing that mattered to him above all else. That was Teague. Jack and Teague may not have always seen eye-to-eye, but that didn't change the fact that they had a very close bond—they were family.

Because of this, Jack could not let himself sit idle while Teague battled, or tried to escape, the navy. He needed to take some sort of action. But he knew that Teague might not be very receptive. After all, Jack had left home in the middle of the night and stowed away on a merchant ship bound for the pirate town of Tortuga. No parent or guardian or person-who-might-be-your-parent would accept that.

Unless he was a pirate.

"Jackie," Teague called out from aboard his ship. The huge reddish boat dwarfed the *Barnacle*. A figurehead of a woman with a

tail for legs decorated its bow, and along the ship's side was the name *Misty Lady*.

Jack looked up. "What?"

"Maybe you've forgotten, but the navy is bringing up the rear. Mighty quick, too."

"What on earth does that have to do with me?" Jack asked, wishing his face was still buried in his knees.

Teague raised an eyebrow and gave Jack a knowing glance. Jack knew exactly what that look meant. No matter where Jack tried to run to, no matter how hard he attempted to escape, he would be inextricably linked to Teague and his pirating ways forever.

"I'm *not* a pirate," Jack said evenly.

"It won't matter much *what* you are if you're blown to bits by a cannon blast, will it?" Teague replied. His men were scurrying across the deck, readying their ship for battle. Jack stood up. The navy was merely a league or so away now. Jack had two options: he could sit in his boat and most likely be barreled over or blown apart by the navy, or he could hop aboard Teague's ship and only less likely be blown apart.

"What makes you think I'm not a match for the navy and their friends?" Jack asked.

Teague laughed quietly. Then he grabbed one of the pirates who was scurrying aboard his ship. The pirate wore a vest but no shirt, and Jack noticed that some of the many tattoos on his arms looked familiar. One of them was the same icon that adorned Teague's Jolly Roger—a skeleton holding a speared heart. The pirate ran his fingers through his spiky black hair as Teague whispered something to him. Then he saluted Teague and rejoined the rest of the crew.

"Remember all those times I needed to step in and come to your rescue?" Teague asked.

"You speak as if you'd *let* me forget," Jack said.

"Well, this is another one of those times," Teague said. Then he motioned to the pirate he had whispered to moments before, and a half-dozen of Teague's men rushed toward the broadside of his great ship. The pirate who Teague had talked to used a small cannon to shoot a line from Teague's ship to the *Barnacle*, and before Jack could make sense of what was going on, Teague's men were aboard the rickety boat.

"We come 'ere to retrieve ya," said the pirate that Teague had whispered to. Now that Jack was standing next to him, he realized the pirate was quite a bit shorter than him. When the man had been standing aboard Teague's huge ship, he looked much taller. Jack had battled some towering captains during his year alone at sea. So he didn't feel all that threatened by this little man. He started to giggle.

"Well, that's a novel idea, mate," Jack said, "But how, pray tell, do you plan on getting us—meaning we, meaning me and you, plus your quintet of jolly pirates here—back up there on board ye ol' ship o' Teague's, while we're all way down yonder on Jack's wee *Barnacle*."

The pirate smirked.

"Well, we got *down* that line, ain't we? So we'll just need to go back up it."

Jack sneered.

"Maybe *you've* got to go up it. Me, however, I have no intention of moving from my ship," Jack said proudly. "Besides, going *up* a line is just a mite more difficult than coming down one," Jack went on, eyeing the scrawny pirate. "So, good luck getting back up there. May the fates be with you, et cetera, et cetera. . . ."

"I've already said yer comin' along," said the pirate. "And Renegade Robbie don't never go back on his word." Then the man lowered his voice and added, "Especially not to Teague, mind you."

"'Renegade Robbie'?" Jack said, barely holding back laughter. "That has got to be the stupidest—" But before he could finish, Renegade Robbie delivered a fierce blow to his midsection, and Jack found himself laid out on the deck. Jack had been hit so hard, he felt like he was going to vomit. He looked up at the pirate. There was no way a man of such slight size could pack such a punch. Jack caught his breath and leaped to his feet. Though he was still in a great deal of pain, he rushed Robbie, who, without hesitation and with great ease, clenched his fist and threw another punch. This one landed Jack on his rear end and sent him skidding toward the

Barnacle's railing. Jack tried to comprehend the situation. It was clear this little guy was stronger than he looked.

"Now, are ya thinkin' ya'll be comin' along wit' us? Or, we gonna have ta force ya a bit more?" Robbie said. The five other members of Teague's crew who had joined Robbie stood behind him. Though they were much larger than Robbie, Jack felt less threatened by them. After all, it was clear that it was Robbie who packed the biggest wallop.

Jack shrugged. "Well, seeing as I have no other option . . ."

"I knew ya'd come around," Robbie said.

Jack threw his arms up in submission, but as Robbie reached out to grab him, Jack drew his sword and started slashing. Robbie whipped out twin daggers and stabbed at Jack.

"Don't hurt him," Teague bellowed from the deck of his ship.

Robbie immediately pulled back.

"Well, why didn't ya tell me that before?" Robbie asked. "I think I already done some damage to 'im."

Before Robbie could continue his dialogue with Teague, Jack swiped at him with his sword, grazing his spiky hair and leaving him with an almost-bald patch. Jack jumped on the railing and smirked at Robbie. Robbie's first instinct was to throw a fist at Jack, but Teague cleared his throat loudly, and Robbie checked himself.

"Now look, boy," Robbie said, "we ain't wanting no difficulty. We just want ya to come along all nice-like. We's only looking out for your own good."

"Oh, *my own good!* It's all clear now. Had you said so in the first place, I would have gladly joined you aboard your mighty vessel. Except, now wait a minute . . . does your idea of 'my own good' entail pirating, looting, and family gatherings where everyone is very keen on playing 'pin the tail on Jack'? Yes, yes, I can tell by the look on your face that that's exactly what you have in mind, so, sorry mate, I am going to have to sadly decline your offer, and, further, ask you to leave my ship," Jack said, folding his arms in defiance.

Renegade Robbie looked puzzled. "So," he said to Teague, "not really sure what to do now . . . ummm . . . ya did, after all, ask me not to hurt 'im, but at the same time ya asked me to come an' fetch 'im, too. Pardon, Captain, but, errr, it might be difficult to do both."

Teague was clearly growing impatient, and Jack noticed his all-too-familiar temper flaring up.

"Listen to me," Teague said through

clenched teeth. "We have a fleet of warships that want to blow us out of the sea, and they are nary a league behind us. If the boy wants to stay aboard his boat, let him. But the rest of you, return to the ship."

Jack smiled, satisfied with the way things seemed to be turning out.

Robbie shrugged. "Okay, then." He shook Jack's hand. "It was nice knowing ya. A pity to see such a promising pirate perish at so young an age!"

"First of all, I am not a pirate," Jack said. "And, further, and perhaps more important, it is ever quite presumptuous of you to assume that I am about to die."

Suddenly, a huge cannon blast rocked the serene sea just a half mile from the *Barnacle* and Teague's ship. Jack yelped. Robbie winked and Jack smiled sheepishly.

"So, err," Jack stuttered uncomfortably,

"that offer you extended moments ago. You know, the one about coming aboard your ship and looking out for my best interest and whatnot?"

Robbie's smile widened.

"I assume that offer still stands . . ." Jack finished.

Without answering, Robbie fastened a line around his own waist, then another around Jack's. He indicated to the other pirates who had joined him that they should reboard their own ship, and, turning to Jack again, he tightened the line around his waist, and said, "We've not a moment to lose, mate."

CHAPTER FOUR

$\mathcal{T}$eague seemed remarkably calm for a man who had the combined forces of the Royal Navy and the East India Trading Company on his tail. While Teague never looked back to see how close his pursuers were, Jack was keeping a close eye on the fleet as it continued to make its way toward them.

Teague and Jack sat in silence for a while, as the *Misty Lady* sailed on. Then Jack, having had enough of the intolerable quiet, broke the ice. "So, we just going to sit here? No 'good to see you Jackie, how've you been' and whatnot?" Jack said.

"Jackie, you know I was never one to think that anybody was too young for a pirate's life. It was never your age I was opposed to—you just weren't ready," Teague said.

"Oh, here we go again!" Jack shouted, throwing up his arms. "For your information, I did not *leave* your little shotgun shack in order to go pirating, I left so I would not have to ever think or hear about the vile acts of pirates ever again for as long as I lived. Here you are just thinking 'Jackie's not good enough to be a pirate, why can't he be more like his cousin Valerie, or Grandmama, proper pirates they be, aye matey' and whatnot, but I was never good at it because I didn't want to be—"

"I *never* said anything about you not being

good at it, I just said you weren't ready," Teague repeated.

"Well, six of this, half a dozen of that, isn't it?"

"No. They're two very different things. You have it in you—more than anyone I have ever known. And you know how many pirates I have seen come and go. When I said you weren't ready, I meant that—"

But before Teague could finish, another cannonball erupted beside the *Misty Lady*.

"All hands!" Teague commanded. His crew shuffled quickly around the deck, readying their positions. Most steadied themselves behind cannons, preparing their ammunition, while the rest checked their muskets.

"It's not like them to fire warning shots," Teague mused.

As if in response, the fleet began to send a full-on barrage of cannonballs toward the

Misty Lady. Teague's crew returned it in kind, and soon the entire sea was covered in such a thick, gray cloud of gun smoke that Jack couldn't tell where the attack was coming from. The smoke was blocking out the sun. The only light came from the explosive flashes of cannon fire, which flickered and flashed like strange orange lightning.

Jack had seen a lot since he'd left home. But he'd never seen anything quite like this. His closest point of reference was when the *Barnacle* had been transformed into a hulking warship called the *Grand Barnacle*, and he had gone head-to-head with one navy warship.* But even that single navy vessel had caused an unimaginably loud and chaotic scene. Yet it paled in comparison to the violent roar of the exploding cannons from the attacking fleet.

*Back in Vol. 4, *The Sword of Cortés*.

Jack looked at Teague. His jaw was set and he looked determined, but he also looked confident. It was as if he somehow knew that he would emerge victorious from this seemingly impossible situation. Jack just thought this was further evidence that the man was mad.

Then something caught Jack's eye, tearing him away from his reverie. Out on the water, he noticed a shadowy silhouette sailing among the swirling smoke clouds. At first he thought it might be a wayward fishing boat that had been pulled into the battle. Leaning closer, he squinted his eyes to get a better look, coughing violently to clear his lungs of the heavy weight of the gunpowder he'd been inhaling. His eyes were tearing, making it even more difficult to discern the exact figure of the boat, but for a moment he thought it must be the *Barnacle* sailing away.

The heat of the battle's getting to you, Jack, he said to himself. Then he turned north, the direction in which he had left the *Barnacle*. Though he couldn't see through the thick smoke, he knew that the area was likely now filled with navy ships firing away, and that a small boat like the *Barnacle* would never be able to withstand such a violent attack. He hung his head, remembering his lost ship. He wanted to observe a moment of silence. But he found this to be completely impossible.

"Can somebody please just lower the volume on those cannons? I feel something oozing from my ears, and whereas I would usually just assume it to be runny ear wax, I am fairly certain it is the telltale blood of broken eardrums!" Jack shouted.

As if in response, the firing quieted down considerably, before dissolving into only sporadic eruptions and then finally settling down into an eerie calm.

Jack's eyes popped open a bit. His ears were ringing so loudly that they hurt.

"What do we do now?" he asked.

"Now we wait," Teague responded, still looking confident.

"Well, if you don't mind my asking, what is it that we're waiting for?"

Teague rolled his eyes, then turned to Jack. "Jackie, do you remember Sven the Vicious?"

Jack wrinkled his nose and thought hard. He ran through his mental catalogue of his family and their fellow pirates.

"Short guy? Sort of a little bit drunk all the time?"

"No, that was Steven the Vicious— Sven . . ."

"Ah, yes, now I recall. Norwegian fellow. Made quite a good *rakfisk*. I liked it very much, even though I never really was one for fermented fish."

"You've got it now, lad. That was him. Do you remember what *happened* to Sven, Jackie?" Teague asked, leaning in toward Jack.

Jack thought for a moment. "They didn't force him into servitude as a cook on a navy vessel, where he would be forbidden to ever prepare that lovely *rakfisk* again, did they?"

"Almost as terrible," Teague said. "They hanged him at the docks of Port Royal, under a huge sign that read, *Pirates, Be Ye Warned!*"

"Er, who is 'ye' and what should he be warned of?" Jack asked.

"Jackie," Teague said, exasperated, "be warned or ye—meaning whosoever reads the sign—shall suffer the same fate as Sven, and Black-Eyed Susan, and Captain Lawrence Schaefer. Which were all executed in the same way—hanged—for all to see, Jackie."

"Oh. Oh, well, that's not very pleasant is it? Still, I wonder. How should this make me feel any more comfortable about our current situation?" Jack asked.

Teague smiled. "It means that no matter how much of a show they were putting on just now, they would never take me, or any of my men, anything but alive. They want the pleasure of killing us themselves. They want to use us for exemplary punishment. And that always gives us an edge over them, understand?"

"Exemplawhat?" Jack began, then stopped midsentence and gulped.

Standing right behind Teague was a tall man in a navy uniform. He had sneaked on so quietly that it was as though he had appeared from thin air. Jack looked to the far end of the ship and noticed that there was a reason the cannon fire had stopped. Officers from one of the vessels were slipping into skiffs and traveling through the thick smoke over to the *Misty Lady*, then climbing aboard.

"Shackle every one of these low-life scoundrels, bring them aboard, and lock them in the brig," shouted the first man to have arrived on board. From his uniform, he appeared to be an admiral. His men held their muskets to the crew and forced them to drop their own weapons. Then, the officers moved to chain up the pirates.

"Leave him to me," the admiral said, motioning to Teague. "I've waited a very long time for this."

"Lawrence Norrington, commanding admiral of this fleet, I presume," Teague said as his hands were being shackled.

"Well, well, it would appear even a dim-witted scoundrel like you is capable of being correct on occasion," the admiral replied.

Jack's arms were pulled tightly behind

him as two members of the navy secured them with rope. Admiral Norrington walked over to Jack. "And as for you . . . we've been keeping track of you for months now. You are quite a pirate in the making. We'll put an end to that very quickly."

"I am *not* a pi—" Jack began. But before he could finish, Norrington clapped his hands twice, indicating to his crew that the captives should be taken from the *Misty Lady* and brought aboard his vessel.

"I think this situation is what one might call a 'pickle'," Jack said nervously.

"Mmmm, pickles be tasty sometimes," Renegade Robbie said, as he was shuffled past Jack and forced off Teague's ship.

CHAPTER FIVE

*E*very inch of Jack's clothing was soaked.
The stinging Caribbean saltwater dripped
from his sopping bandana and was running in
tiny streams over his forehead and settling in
his eyes. He wished his hands were not tied
behind his back so that he would be able to
remove the bandana and wring it out.

He, along with Teague's crew, had been
tossed overboard. Then, like the others, he'd
been fished from the water by navy crewmen

who were waiting alongside the *Misty Lady* in rowboats to collect their prisoners. Now the pirates were lying on top of one another like sopping-wet sardines in an open can.

Most of the crew had been tossed into the large rowboat where Jack found himself. But Teague was taken to the admiral's skiff. When he craned his neck at a right angle, Jack could see the other boat, mere feet away from his own. It was being rowed by one of the admiral's men and contained two other guards, each pointing his musket at the captain's skull.

Jack heaved a sigh. Since leaving home, he had been on adventures that would have made an ordinary boy his age cringe. He had felt so free commanding the *Barnacle*, he had felt powerful and clever when he'd outwitted the merfolk,* but right now, in what was

*In Vol. 4, *The Sword of Cortés.*

probably the most dangerous moment in his short career at sea, he felt very small, like a child who needed to be watched after. He turned his gaze toward Teague again, resenting him for churning up all these unwanted feelings.

Jack squirmed a little bit to get more comfortable and wound up shifting into a position where a soggy boot was right in his face. It smelled like a mixture of spoiled milk and cow manure.

"While I would love to inhale your rotten cheese-smelling boots during the length of the ride, it might be prudent of you to move them before I regurgitate my last meal all over the lot of you," Jack said, straining to see the person to whom he was talking.

"Sorry, mate." It was Robbie, and as he shifted to move himself away from Jack, he must have kicked a number of other sailors, as shouts of disgust, moans, and groans followed while he adjusted his position.

"Oh, it was you," Jack said.

"Aye," Robbie replied. "No worries, though, mate. Judging from the last three or four times we've taken a trip over to u'navy vessel, we should only be on this raft a li'l bit longer."

"How many times have you been taken by the navy, exactly?" Jack asked, not surprised that Teague and his men had managed to escape multiple captures.

"Oh, a dozen or so. Too many to keep track of. Never been quite this many of 'em though. Usually just a boat or two. Perhaps a trio here and there. Methinks they mean business this time," Robbie explained.

"And yet the lot of you seem unfazed by this," said Jack.

"Well, you know, Teague, 'e 'as a way of

getting out of these things," Robbie answered.

"But don't you ever consider that there'll be a time when he—and you—yous, I mean, will not be able to pull off a quick-and-easy escape?" Jack asked.

"Never considered that," Robbie said thoughtfully.

"Well, that seems unwise," Jack replied.

"Why's that?" Robbie asked, sounding almost indignant. "I mean, if we don't get out of it, it probably means we're dead, and if that's the case, we won't have any need to worry 'bout these things anyway, because, well, we'll be, um, dead."

There was a certain ironic brilliance to this, and Jack was too moved to respond. Then there was a sudden jerk. It felt like the skiff had slammed into a brick wall.

"Ah! Thar' we are! We've 'it the ship," Robbie announced.

Jack groaned as the crew was pulled a man at a time from the tiny boat. Each time someone was yanked out, the others would shift, and by the time Jack was removed from the boat, his arms and legs had been twisted so much that they were practically knotted up with the limbs of four other pirates.

Jack was loaded—along with the other men—onto a platform that was connected to a pulley bolted to the deck. They were piled on top of each other, squirming for air and shouting at one another as they were lifted aboard the navy vessel and unceremoniously dumped onto the deck. Once they were all aboard, the navy officers lined them up and then lowered the platform once again.

The rusty pulleys screeched as they ground against rusty hinges and began to lift the platform back to the deck.

As Jack and the others looked on, the

curly top of a man's head appeared, just over the balustrade. The navy crew pulled harder and harder, and the man came into fuller view. It was as if he were levitating alongside the ship. Then his face became visible to Jack. It was Teague. He still looked resolute, but now there was a clear anger on his face as well. The officers on deck kept on hauling till he was level with the balustrade. Then they grabbed him by his bound legs and pulled him off the platform, sending him crashing to the deck.

Following behind him was Admiral Lawrence Norrington. He hurried over to Teague with a fierce determination.

He leaned down and unceremoniously dragged Teague to his feet.

"The previous time you evaded us was surely the last," the admiral said. "Make fast for Tortuga," he commanded.

"Admiral, are you sure that's—" an officer began to question.

"What this *is*, Lewis, is an *order*," the admiral said sternly through clenched teeth.

"Aye, sir," the officer said, saluting.

Then the admiral turned back toward Teague. He stuck his sword beneath Teague's chin, forcing the pirate to look him in the eyes.

"There is no better place to deter piracy than in its safest haven in the Caribbean. Tortuga is a pirate town, rampant with your kind, filled with misery and corruption. You'll enjoy your final visit there, I am sure. It will last mere minutes, and then you'll be hanging from the gallows, on display for all to see—a warning to those who might dare follow in your footsteps."

With these last few words, the admiral shot Jack a warning glance.

"We've been down this road before, haven't we?" Teague said.

The admiral looked back at Teague with utter disdain. Then he scowled and spat swiftly in the pirate's face.

"Take them all to the brig," the admiral ordered. "Lock them up until we make landfall in Tortuga. As for him—" The admiral motioned to Teague. "—throw him in the same brig as the rest of the common slime. Now that he's aboard, there's no need to administer special treatment to this sea slug."

Jack and the rest of the crew, with Teague in front, were marched belowdecks and thrown into the brig. The men each had less than a foot of space between them, and as the gate was closed by the guard, Jack heard an unearthly howl coming from the far end of the cell. One of the pirate's hands had been crushed in the gate as the guard was closing it. The pirate held his broken, limp hand by the wrist.

Jack craned his neck to see if it was anyone he recognized, but he hadn't seen this particular pirate before. It was easy to lose track of the men, though, as Teague had a pretty large crew. Above the man's cries, Jack heard the jiggle of the keys and the click of the lock. The man's cries settled down into sobs, and a few minutes later, the only other sound was the steady beat of the guards' footsteps as they walked away from the brig.

When the footsteps had died away, Jack turned to Robbie, who had been squished in next to him. "Well, what do you usually do now?" Jack asked, knowing that Robbie had been in this situation before.

"Usually we just wait, mate. Hey, that rhymed, did'n't?" the pirate said.

Jack rolled his eyes.

"How *long* do you wait for?" Jack asked.

"That depends. Been in 'ere a week once. 'Nother time it was nothin' but a few hours. Sometimes this nice doggie comes by, and he usually got the keys we need to get out."* Suddenly there was a loud yelp from the far end of the brig.

"Ye stepped on me foot, ye dolt."

Jack could not see whose foot had been so ruthlessly stomped upon, but the fellow sounded quite irate about it.

"Who ye callin' a dolt? Ye dolt!" another voice called out in response.

"Why ye . . . I'll murder ye."

"I'll murder ye pet doggie," yet another voice rang out.

"Don't ye be talkin' about Bessie like that," still another called.

*Jack had his own run-in with this wonder dog in Vol. 5: *The Age of Bronze.*

"Well, I don't much like the color of yer bandana, mate."

By this time, Jack had completely lost track of who was talking to whom. But it was clear to him that the argument had begun to spread through the brig. Then it happened. Jack felt a wave of pirates swell over him, and he was pushed backward and forced to hop on his bound legs. Before he knew it, pirates seemed to have freed themselves from their bonds, and a brawl was breaking out in the very tight space of the brig.

Suddenly Jack's face was thrust into the rusted iron grating as the pirate next to him fell into Jack.

"Excuse me, sir," Jack said politely, "most of you seem to have managed to wiggle your way out of your bonds. I, however, am having a bit more difficulty."

The pirate, who was at least a foot taller

than Jack, seemed to grow enraged. His face turned bright red and he lifted a mighty hand over his head.

Jack gulped.

And then the pirate brought his fist down upon the bonds around Jack's legs, grabbed at them, and began gnawing right through them! Jack squinted at the bizarre nature of this and then thanked him quickly. The pirate's demeanor did not change, however. He threw Jack violently against the wall, and with another cry of what sounded like vicious rage, he began to chew away at the ties that bound Jack's hands.

When the pirate was done snacking, Jack had to admit he was happy to be free of his bonds. He was suffering from some rope burns around his wrists—not to mention some teeth marks. With one last grunt, the large, angry pirate plowed through the crowded brig and, like a battering ram, slammed himself into the gate, succeeding only in bruising his forehead.

Jack smirked.

The chaos increased as pirates began swinging at anything that moved. Jack ducked a few blows and at one point spotted Teague standing apart from the commotion, smoking a pipe with a leg up against the brig's grating. He had not been touched by the havoc and didn't seem the slightest bit phased by it.

Then, a shout erupted from outside the brig.

"Stop it all, right now, or we'll hang the lot of ye, we will!"

The crowd in the brig settled down. Jack noticed a look of recognition on Teague's face at the sound of the voice. Teague began slowly pushing his way toward the front of the brig. When he got there, he looked the man on the other side straight in the face and smiled.

"Well, well, if it's not Mr. Joshamee Gibbs," Teague said.

"At your service, sir," the man said, straightening his navy uniform and smiling back.

CHAPTER SIX

$\mathcal{J}$ack was surprised to see Teague talking to
a navy officer, and even more surprised that
the navy officer was talking back, and *most*
surprised that the navy officer was smiling
at Teague!

"What in heaven's name is going on
here?" Jack asked.

"What'cha mean?" Renegade Robbie
asked. He had made his way over to Jack's
side when the brawl had settled down. For
all his part in the fight, Robbie seemed to be

largely unscathed, save a tiny bump over his left eye.

"Teague—navy officer—talking—nicey nice . . . explain," Jack said.

"Oh, right. Well, er, that's Mr. Gibbs."

Jack looked back toward Mr. Gibbs. He didn't look like a pirate, what with his navy uniform and relatively trim sideburns. He was a stout man, with a shock of auburn hair and a face that Jack suspected looked older than it really was. At the same time, he didn't look entirely like a navy officer, either. His sideburns might have been trim for a pirate, but they were a tad bushy for an officer. His uniform looked a bit more disheveled than the rest of the navy crew's, as well.

"So, this Mr. Gibbs," Jack said, "why is he being so nice to the prisoners?"

"Well, ya see," Robbie explained, "Mr.

Gibbs likes to move the drink along—not only down his own hatch, but on the Caribbean, too. Sells it, he does. And we pirates really like our freedom. In addition—as I'm sure ya already knew—we have some connections with the runners down Rumrunners Island. So, let's just say we furnish Mr. Gibbs with an endless supply of something he loves and sells, and he makes sure we stay free to keep on supplying it."

Jack stared blankly at Robbie.

"So, your ability to remain free resides in the hands of a rum trafficker smitten with the drink," Jack said.

"Never thought of it that way . . . but, yeah, I guess that would be correct," Robbie said.

Jack was beginning to realize that being a pirate was less about thinking things through and more about acting on gut instinct.

"Hey, it's worked this far, ain't it?" Robbie pointed out, noticing Jack's expression of disbelief.

Yet again, Jack was unable to argue this point with Robbie. Jack excused himself and made his way toward Teague. When he arrived at his side, Mr. Gibbs's jaw dropped.

"It can't be, can it?" Mr. Gibbs asked.

Jack stared blankly at Mr. Gibbs, who now had a wide smile beaming across his face.

"It can be, if you want it to, but if you don't it might still be, in which case you would be correct, except for the fact that I have no idea what you're talking about, so I find it impossible to confirm. Sorry, mate," Jack replied.

"Aha!" Mr. Gibbs blurted out. "It is! No other boy is so clever. Jackie, last time I saw you, you were yay high." Mr. Gibbs indicated about a meter from the floor with his hand.

"You must be mistaking me for another Jackie what was about yay high last time you saw him, because, I, sir, have never seen you before in my life."

Jack suddenly felt a swift slap upside his head. He looked up to see Teague scowling at him.

"Jackie, is that any way to treat an old family friend?" Teague asked.

Jack squinted at Gibbs. "Ah, yes! Mr. Gibbs! Sure, yes, of course, I remember you now. You were at that—"

"Barbecue!" Mr. Gibbs finished for Jack.

"Yes, yes, that *barbecue* we had down on—"

"Rumrunners Island!" Mr. Gibbs finished again.

"Yes, of course! Where else? We were celebrating—"

"Yer Grandmama's seventy-fourth birthday!"

Jack stopped for a moment then mumbled,

"That old bat has lived thrice as long as she's deserved to."

Jack felt another slap upside his head and knew without looking that it came from Teague.

"Listen, Joshamee," Teague said. "We need to find a way out of here. You're always good on your word, and you know we stay good on ours, if you know what I mean."

"Yes, loyalty—a mighty strange trait for pirates such as yourselves. Still, it's gonna be mighty tricky this time. The admiral has brought his son aboard, for lord-knows-what reason, and security is exceptionally tight," Mr. Gibbs said.

"Joshamee . . ." Teague said slowly and deliberately, "we all know how much you love your rum and the ability to *trade* it . . . and we also know how much it would bother you to lose your endless access to said beverage."

"I *do* love it," Mr. Gibbs said dreamily. "And I love the doubloons it brings me just as well. I am running a tad low at the current time, what with the cost of bribing guards to free pirates constantly increasing and whatnot. . . ."

"Mr. Gibbs," Teague said, sounding very official, "will you be helping us, or will we have to explore other avenues to secure our release?"

Gibbs sighed.

"Let me see what I can do," he said.

"A drunk 'seeing what he can do.' Very reassuring indeed," Jack muttered.

*N*ight had fallen, and the brig had gone dark, with the exception of a few weak shafts of moonlight that made their way through the portholes. The members of Teague's crew were slumped on top of one another, snoring and drooling and kicking one another in their sleep. But Jack was wide awake, his mind racing.

Was this the life he was destined for? Being chased by the authorities and locked up, only to escape and run free, and be chased and locked up yet again, and so on and so forth, ad nauseum? He scanned the room and landed on Teague. Besides Jack, Teague was the only other man in the brig who was awake. He still wore his steadfast expression, and if there was any measure of exhaustion in the man, it wasn't evident. All this running, all this fighting and looting and backstabbing and rebelling—for what?

Before Jack could think about it any more deeply, there was a click at the brig's gate, followed by a hushed order from a man who stood in shadow.

"Wake your men, file out quietly," the

man in the shadows said. Jack looked around. There were at least two dozen men in the brig with him. How would they be able to quietly wake them all and sneak off without being detected?

Teague stood up, looking like a giant among the throngs of sailors who were sleeping on the floor. He cleared his throat rather loudly, and at once the men all but jumped to attention.

"Come now, carefully," the man at the gate whispered, just loud enough for the crew to hear.

Jack was one of the first to file out, and as he passed the man who had unlocked the gate, he realized it was Mr. Gibbs.

"Thank you kindly!" Jack said a little too loudly, bowing. Mr. Gibbs shushed him.

"Hurry, Jackie. You don't have much time," Mr. Gibbs said.

"Funny, that. Very recently, I had all the time in the world, and I didn't want it much,"* Jack responded. Mr. Gibbs gave him a puzzled look and ushered him out of the brig. Renegade Robbie followed close behind. Jack, wearing a suspicious sneer, gave him a sidelong glance.

"You fancy being my shadow, mate?" Jack asked.

"Don't be blamin' me for that," Robbie said. "'Tis Captain Teague what wants me to follow ya."

Jack rolled his eyes. Was he always to be treated like a child?

As the crew moved past another brig, Jack saw what looked like a heap of dirty laundry. Upon closer inspection, he realized that it

---

*Jack is referring to his experience with a watch that could affect time, which he was in possession of not long ago . . . Vol. 8, *The Timekeeper*, and Vol. 9, *Dance of the Hours*, to be exact!

was a group of sailors, unconscious, piled on top of each other.

"Funny what drink can do to a man, ain't it?" Mr. Gibbs said, smiling.

Up on deck, it was utterly silent, and Jack felt almost at ease as the sound of the lapping waves echoed over the ocean, and the bright moonlight played upon the mainsail and sparkled on the little swells.

"Quickly, here," Mr. Gibbs said, nodding to a skiff that was tied to the broadside of the ship. Jack looked around, wondering what the protocol was. Then he decided he had no trouble boarding the boat first. He jumped in, and the boat creaked and slammed against the hull, creating quite a racket. The rest of the crew shot Jack angry glances, and Jack gulped.

"Shush, Jackie, quiet if ya please!" Mr. Gibbs said. "Yer ship is over yonder," he continued, pointing in a vague, northeasterly direction. Jack squinted and could barely make out the *Misty Lady*'s hulking silhouette under the moonlight.

Carefully, the rest of the crew made its way into the skiff.

Mr. Gibbs stood back, and with a salute and a wave of his hat, raised his sword and cut through the lines that were holding the small boat in place.

An instant later, the boat began free-falling toward the water, and Jack let out a girlish scream. The other pirates, who were clutching the sides of the raft, hardly seemed to hear him. Then the boat splashed loudly into the water, soaking the crew, who seemed satisfied that they had escaped.

Jack looked around to survey what they were up against—but most, if not all, of the navy and East India Trading Company ships had gone. It seemed that with Teague captured, the rest of the fleet had withdrawn.

And then Jack's eyes fixed on something. He squinted in an attempt to better see what it was. He quickly found that squinting in the dark was decidedly unhelpful. But as Teague's crew rowed on, Jack knew exactly what it was he was looking at.

"Oh, no. No, no, no, no, and *NO!*" Jack said, very clearly stressing that there was no way in the world that he would believe in any part of what he was seeing.

"What's got ya in a tizzy?" Robbie asked.

Jack just set his jaw and stared in a fixed direction. He was looking at the *Barnacle*. It was anchored not twenty yards away, and on its mast was flying the flag belonging to the East India Trading Company. Jack was incensed.

The East India Trading Company was in the business of trading spices and fine linens. They were also, Jack had recently discovered, in the business of trafficking people—something Jack had absolutely no tolerance for.

Jack also knew that the Company was in league with the Royal Navy and that the two had joined together with the sole goal of wiping pirates off the face of the Earth. A year ago, Jack might have agreed with them. But since setting off on his own, Jack was beginning to have second thoughts about good and evil, piracy and conformity, and, in the world of material things, what, exactly, belonged to whom. . . .

That was his boat. He had found it. He had taken it on adventure after adventure. No one else—no man, no captain, no king, no company—would fly their flag on *his* boat.

Without considering the consequences of what he was about to do, Jack sprang off the longboat, dove into the water, and began to make his way to his beloved *Barnacle*.

CHAPTER SEVEN

*J*ack swam quicker than he ever imagined he could. Under the night sky, the sea looked like one huge, shadowy mass of black liquid, ready to swallow him up. But that was not what kept him going. He needed to get to his boat and reclaim it.

When he reached the *Barnacle*, Jack took a deep breath and climbed onto its deck, using the rope ladder that hung over its side. It felt good to be aboard the *Barnacle* again. Part of him just wanted to raise the anchor and run away—from Teague, from the navy, from the whole blasted Caribbean. But he knew that first he needed to set things straight.

He looked out over the broadside and saw that Teague had stopped rowing his skiff and was looking at the *Barnacle*. For a moment, Jack wondered if Teague would be upset that he had jumped off the longboat. But he quickly put the concerns of others out of his mind and set out to do what he needed to do for himself.

He walked over to the mast, wrapped his legs around it, then climbed up until he could reach the flag of the East India Trading Company. With great satisfaction, he tore the flag down. Then he wiped his face with it and threw it down toward the deck.

But it didn't seem to reach the deck. Instead, it looked as if the flag had fallen onto something that looked very much like a statue. The "statue" quickly whipped the flag from its head, and Jack saw that he was not alone aboard the *Barnacle*.

"Well, well," the figure said. "You have escaped the navy, I see. Might one think it wise to simply flee once they have been granted such an opportunity at freedom? It is what you have always done before."

As he spoke, the figure stepped into a shaft of moonlight, and Jack—who had just lowered himself off the mast—saw that it was his *ex*-crewmember, Fitzwilliam.

Fitzwilliam drew his sword.

"I have been waiting for this moment a long time, Jack," he said. "You have no idea how infuriating it had been for me, sailing aboard your wretched little boat, taking *your* orders."

"I think I have some sort of an idea," Jack said. "After all, I was quite disgusted just having you *aboard*. And you may have thought you had me fooled, but I say 'the pigeons,' Fitzy, the *pigeons!*"

Fitzwilliam snarled. "You are as mad as ever. What in the good earth's name are you talking about?"

"Oh, don't play dodo bird with me, Fitz," Jack said casually. "I remember a number of occasions while we were sailing with nothing much else going on, and you were playing around with birds, talking to them all daintily, like you were some princess in a fairy tale. You even mentioned that your father was a sort of a birder,* which I thought was an odd hobby for an aristocrat. You, however, had it all planned out. I knew something was amiss, and I was on the verge of finding out exactly what it was, when your Royal Navy and East India Trading

*In Vol. 9, *Dance of the Hours*.

Company pals dropped in on us.

"Those birds were carrying messages to your lads over there, weren't they?" Jack continued. "You were tracking my moves. Thing is, in the end, it wasn't you or your spying or the birdies that found Teague. It was the navy and the Company. Without your help. All you succeeded in doing was bringing Teague and me together again, and I'd say that that was purely coincidence."

Fitzwilliam sneered.

"But had you not run away, Teague would not have been searching for you—and hence would not have run afoul of the navy," Fitzwilliam said flatly.

"Who says he was looking for me, mate?" Jack asked.

"Regardless," Fitzwilliam said, "in the process of sailing with you, I have come to know you and your tricks and your pirate friends. And to that end, I believe I have delivered a more valuable pirate than even Teague. You are wily, smarmy, and untrustworthy, Jack Sparrow."

"Why, thank you," Jack replied. "I do believe that's the kindest compliment you've ever paid me."

"And if you think that I am going to allow you to flee, after having just captured you, you are sadly mistaken."

Fitzwilliam raised his sword, and Jack drew his. In moments, the two boys were clashing, their weapons clanking away, glistening under the pale moonlight. Jack quickly jumped on a barrel in which the crew had kept salted fish and was immediately followed by Fitzwilliam, who sprang up on the balustrade. Fitzwilliam swung at Jack's legs, and Jack jumped, just barely avoiding the swipe.

Jack jumped backward off of the barrel, landing on the deck. He grabbed a ballast and swung it above his head multiple times to gain momentum. Then he let it fly, and it struck Fitzwilliam directly in the gut. Fitzwilliam fell to the deck, and Jack rushed over to him and pointed his sword at Fitzwilliam's neck. A small smirk spread across his lips as he stood over the other boy.

"I hope you do not believe it would be so easy to overcome me," Fitzwilliam said. Steadying himself with his arms, he quickly pushed himself out from underneath Jack. Fitzwilliam jumped up and began another fierce assault, relentlessly swiping away at Jack.

"How ever did you come in possession of this ship, anyway, Fitzy?" Jack said casually, acting as if he were not on the receiving end of a full-on assault.

"Some advice: in the future, check the waters around your boat before you decide that the man you have sent overboard is done for. I simply spent some time clinging to this disgusting little vessel before reclaiming it once you had abandoned ship."

"Would you mind terribly answering why you want it so badly if it's such a disgusting vessel," Jack retorted, even as he fended off Fitzwilliam's blows.

"For evidence, of course. It will be slightly more difficult convicting a boy of your age of piracy than someone of, say, Teague's stature and renown," Fitzwilliam said.

For some reason this made Jack furious. He began to let loose on Fitzwilliam like a berserker.

"For the last blasted time," Jack said, "I am not a pirate. I am not going to be convicted of anything, for I am guilty of nothing, and

I want you to get off my ship, for *good!*"

"And I will tell *you* for the last time," Fitzwilliam said, "that I am taking this ship in as evidence. I am taking *you* back where you belong—specifically, to the brig of Admiral Norrington's ship, and, if I can manage, I will alert them to the fact that your supposed father is on the run yet again."

The two boys fought furiously. It was unlike the bickering and bantering that Jack and Fitzwilliam had engaged in during their adventures on the Seven Seas. This was filled with venom and animosity and rage— from both sides.

Fitzwilliam lunged and took a swing at Jack, shredding the edges of his bandana. Jack was relieved that Fitzwilliam had missed his neck, but still felt that the blow was a little too close for comfort.

Jack jumped into the rigging, holding fast to it with one hand, while battling away Fitzwilliam with the other. And then it happened. Fitzwilliam hit Jack with a blow that knocked Jack's sword right out of his hand. Now Jack was weaponless, facing Fitzwilliam who was in possession of both of their swords.

"Now, Fitzy, let's calm down. Remember all the good times we've had together? Mermaids, pirates, storm kings . . ." Jack said.

"Oh, do not even attempt to—" Fitzwilliam began.

But before he could finish, Jack had taken the opportunity provided by the brief pause for conversation and tackled Fitzwilliam. Fitzwilliam's sword flew from his hand, though he was still holding on to Jack's. Reaching out, Jack grabbed Fitzwilliam's

sword, and once again armed, the two continued to spar.

"Well, now I know why you're such an expert swordsman," Jack said, "quite a lot easier to parry with this sword than the old rusty one I've been working with all this time."

It was true. Jack could tell that Fitz-william's ability to spar was significantly lessened while he was holding Jack's sword. Jack's ability, however, felt near perfect with Fitzwilliam's sword in his hand. Jack felt as though he were battling in a manner that was superior to Fitzwilliam's at his best.

And his insights were soon validated.

After some minutes of intense sparring, Jack was able to knock the sword from Fitzwilliam's hand. He had Fitzwilliam on the ground, his foot upon his chest. Jack was glowing. He was triumphant. He had won back his ship, and better yet, he had this mutinous traitor at his disposal and could deal with the situation however he saw fit.

He thought back to the very first time he had met Fitzwilliam and how the aristocrat—if that part of Fitzwilliam's story were even true—had won his place aboard the *Barnacle*.* Jack could not deny that he had begun to, if not trust, then, at the very least, accept Fitzwilliam's presence aboard his boat. All that, and now this outright betrayal.

Worse than a betrayal, really. After all, Jack had been monitored and watched and spied upon for months.

He decided that throwing Fitzwilliam overboard was letting him off easy.

Jack lifted his sword, and an expression of terror formed on Fitzwilliam's face. Even in

*In Vol. 1, *The Coming Storm*.

the moonlight, Jack could see that Fitzwilliam had gone pale. Jack smirked.

But when he went to bring down his sword, the most peculiar thing happened. Jack found that he was unable to move his arm.

He tried and tried, but something was preventing him from doing so.

Then he felt a tugging on his arm.

He turned slowly and found Teague standing there. The captain's hand was clenched tightly around Jack's wrist.

"I don't think that would be the best idea, Jackie," Teague said.

"Yes, well, he stole my boat," Jack said.

"And you took it from someone else," Teague reminded him.

"It was abandoned!" Jack screamed back.

"And so it was." Teague nodded. "Well, it might just be that men like this aristocratic fop over here have different ideas about property and possessing it than men like you and me."

"Well, that's all well and fine, except I am *not* like you!" Jack said.

Teague gave Jack a knowing glance.

"Besides, Fitzwilliam *betrayed* me," Jack said, grasping at straws now.

"Betrayal is another concept that men like him think differently about than men like us. Do you know how many times I've been betrayed by members of my crew?" Teague asked.

"Can't say I do," Jack said flatly.

"Well, neither do I. But it's been quite a lot. Half the men I am sailing with now have at one time or another turned against me for the sake of their own interests. It's what we do. Savvy?" Teague said.

Fitzwilliam, noticing the similarity in Teague and Jack's speech, was not going to let an opportunity to take a dig pass him by.

"I say—if ever there were two pirates more similar . . ."

"Oh, shut up!" Teague and Jack shouted at Fitzwilliam simultaneously.

"So, if we're not going to feed him to the fishies," Jack said, "then what do we do with him?"

"Leave that to me," Teague said with a devilish grin.

CHAPTER EIGHT

$\mathcal{T}$eague's crew had made it back to the *Misty Lady*, and Teague and Jack were on their own. Well, mostly on their own. They still had Fitzwilliam to contend with. This posed a problem, but it was hardly an insurmountable one. Teague had faced deadly enemies and been captured by the Royal Navy many times. But he was still standing. So he found it very humorous to now be on the receiving end of a so-called threat from a teenaged spy.

"If either of you dare touch me, the entire Royal Navy will bear down on you," Fitzwilliam said.

"They already tried that bearing stuff," Jack said jauntily. "Didn't seem to work too well, did it? Seems me and Teague both have got our ships back now, and we're going to soon be on our way without a single hair on our heads singed."

"Of all the arrogant—" Fitzwilliam began.

"Be silent!" Teague commanded. And the authority with which he delivered the order was so severe that even Jack shivered a little bit.

Fitzwilliam fell silent. Jack envied Teague for a moment. He had never been able to make the supposed aristocrat keep his mouth shut for even the shortest period of time.

"Now, you are going to go belowdecks and stay there until we return to this boat. At that point, Jackie will determine how he sees fit to deal with you," Teague said evenly.

Fitzwilliam's expression looked pained. He snarled in resistance but eventually made his way to the door on the deck and descended.

Jack's eyes popped. His jaw hung slack. He knew Teague had a lot of influence— over other pirates and maybe even over some of the more corrupt members of the East India Trading Company and Royal Navy. But Jack had never seen Fitzwilliam behave like this before, and he was certain that there was more than Teague's intimidating demeanor at work here. Fitzwilliam was not one to bow to anyone's commands.

"How on earth did you—" Jack began.

"Never mind," Teague answered. "Now, it's high time I board the *Misty Lady* and make us all scarce. Mind terribly giving me a lift?"

Jack smiled, and grabbed the *Barnacle*'s wheel. It felt good to be in control of her again. Teague unfurled the sails and a strong evening wind filled them, propelling the *Barnacle* closer to the *Misty Lady*. Jack found himself caught up in the tranquil sound of the water rippling around his boat as it sailed on.

Then, *BOOM!* A large cannonball landed just short of the *Barnacle*, rocking it and splashing seawater over the sides.

Jack yelped and looked toward where the cannonball had come from. Admiral Norrington was clearly visible on the deck of his ship. He had spotted the *Barnacle* and commanded his men to open fire upon it.

"Jackie, come now," Teague ordered. "And bring that snot-nosed aristocrat with you!"

"What?" Jack asked, indignant. "Where

are we going, and why would I ever bring him anywhere? Can't we just let him drown?"

"We will need him. Trust might not be the first thing that comes to mind when you hear the name Teague—but trust me anyway," Teague replied. "He'll do whatever you tell him, for the time being anyway. We are headed onto Norrington's ship."

"Oh, that's a very smart idea, isn't it?" Jack asked sarcastically.

"It seems there will be no getting rid of the navy unless we rough them up a little bit," Teague winked. "Go get that rich boy, now!"

Jack cocked an eyebrow. What was Teague on about this time? He walked over to the door that led belowdecks and barked down the stairwell, "Fitzy, come up here, we're abandoning ship!"

To Jack's surprise, Fitzwilliam quickly appeared on deck.

"You OK, mate?" Jack asked.

Fitzwilliam just growled back.

Jack leaned back suspiciously and eyed his former crewmate and current betrayer with suspicion.

"Let's go!" Teague said.

"Let's go!" Jack repeated to Fitzwilliam.

The three jumped from the *Barnacle* and swam quickly over to Norrington's ship as cannon fire erupted all around them. They finally made their way to the ship's ladder, which hung off the broadside, and the three of them ascended to the deck.

The crew was so preoccupied with firing upon the *Barnacle* and readying their guns for the *Misty Lady* that they did not notice the trio climb aboard. Teague motioned toward Jack, indicating to him that he should follow, and Jack did the same thing in turn to Fitzwilliam. Jack could not figure out why

Fitzwilliam hadn't given Jack and Teague away, or why he was following his every order. But he figured that now was not the time to look a gift horse in the mouth.

Within moments, Teague located a room full of weaponry. He furnished himself with two swords, then threw another two to Jack. Jack considered Fitzwilliam for a moment but decided not to include him. After all, Fitzwilliam did have his own shiny sword to spar with.

"Go out and perform reconnaissance," Teague said.

"Are you mad?" Jack snapped back.

"Not you, Jackie . . . you." Teague nodded toward Fitzwilliam.

Fitzwilliam left the room, and Jack stared at Teague.

"Do you mind telling me what's going on here, because I am quite positive that this is not normal behavior on Fitzy's part," Jack said.

Teague shushed Jack and quickly pulled him behind what looked like a barrel of gunpowder. Someone was coming! The door creaked open and Admiral Lawrence Norrington entered. Trailing closely behind him, hanging on to his coattails, was a young boy, about ten years younger than Jack.

"James," Admiral Norrington said, "please refrain from tugging upon my waistcoat."

The boy looked down, ashamed. He was clearly frightened by all the goings-on aboard the ship, and every time a blast resounded he attempted to hide behind the admiral, who, in turn, was having none of it. The admiral squatted beside the boy and held him by the shoulders.

"You need to be brave, son. There are men out there who are savages, and they want to destroy you and your entire way of life. They are uncivilized, heathen, thieving, filthy pirates, and when I have gone on to a final rest, it is you who will carry on the banner of civility and order, and help the Crown and our allies in the East India Trading Company eradicate their slime from the Seven Seas."

As if in response, just as the admiral finished, a tremendous explosion rocked the boat. The boy began to sob, and his father slapped him across the face, telling him to come to his senses and act like a man.

Officers flooded the ammunitions store, all shouting simultaneously. Norrington quickly called for order, the men quieted down, and soon all that could be heard was the boy's sobbing.

"Now, Lieutenant Shepherd, a full report," said the admiral.

A distinguished-looking man in uniform stepped forward and clicked his heels together.

"Sir, our bowsprit's been hit by cannon fire from the *Misty Lady*. We are not sure how much damage was sustained," the man reported.

Norrington looked enraged. "Well, then, why are you all standing here. Go! Survey the damage! And then storm the *Misty Lady* and retrieve for me that lowlife, Captain Teague, and his pint-sized protégé."

Protégé? Jack scowled, taking great offense.

Just then the small room's door swung open once more.

"There will be no need for that, good sirs," a familiar voice filled the room.

Teague cringed and tried to mouth something to Jack. Then the pirate started to gesticulate wildly, but Jack couldn't tell if he were telling him to hide himself more thoroughly or jump up and run out of the room.

Before Jack could decide what to do, he felt someone grabbing him by the hair and pulling him out of his hiding place behind the barrel.

Jack craned his neck and saw Fitzwilliam. He was obviously not beholden to whatever Teague or Jack demanded of him any longer.

"Your captives are here, gentlemen," he said. "And I believe you owe me a great many doubloons—and even more respect—for their safe delivery."

Jack heard the cocking of what sounded like a thousand rifles which were soon pointed directly at him and Teague.

Outside, dawn was breaking over the Caribbean, and Jack was certain he would not live to see the noonday sun.

CHAPTER NINE

"*I* would not hesitate to send you to Davy Jones's Locker right now," Admiral Norrington said flatly. The boy alongside him shivered, evidently startled by the guns and the sudden appearance of two pirates. Jack realized that with all the terrible stories the admiral had been feeding the boy about pirates, the child must have been terrified of him and Teague. This gave Jack the brilliant idea to screw up his nose, make his eyes go all evil, and bare his teeth, causing the boy to jump and grip the admiral's coat before shrinking away from Jack and his startling countenance.

"Someone without hesitation would have done away with us already, would they not have?" Teague asked evenly.

Stifling a roar of rage, the admiral grabbed one of his men's bayonets and jabbed its blade beneath Teague's chin.

"As I can't trust you not to escape before we arrive in Tortuga, we shall have to make do with the means for execution at our disposal here and now. Germaine!" the admiral barked.

"Yes, sir!" A heavyset sailor leaped to the admiral's side.

"Wake the remaining crew and call them to the forecastle. Shepherd, march these two poor excuses for men to the deck."

Then he turned and looked down at the

boy. "James, come with me. You are about to witness something I pray you will never forget."

With those words ringing in their ears, Jack and Teague were shoved toward the stairs leading to the deck. The admiral and his men followed close behind them, with the frightened boy tagging along.

"Move out quicker, or I'll slam you in the kisser," a particularly surly officer shouted, nudging Jack in the back with the butt of a musket.

"I'm deeply flattered, but you're not quite my type," Jack replied.

"Move it!" the officer barked, batting Jack in the backside with the gun.

They emerged onto the deck where the crew had gathered, mostly in their night-clothes. A few officers were recovering from the powerful grip sleep recently held over them, nodding off and yawning loudly. The admiral pushed through the men, dragging the boy behind him like a rag doll.

"Gentlemen, my wish was that we would have had the luxury of performing this act in its appropriate place—the landing at Tortuga. But luxuries and wishes are things reserved for the idle-minded and slothful. Were it the natural order of things—"

"Oh, silence yer muzzle and get on with it, will ye?" a voice shouted out, and Jack was certain that it was Mr. Gibbs.

A few chuckles erupted from the crowd. The admiral looked furious but remained decidedly steadfast in his resolve. He cleared his throat and continued, "As I was saying, were it the natural order of things to have men dress like—ahem—" He nodded disgustedly toward Jack and Teague. "We would be living in a world swarming with flies and overrun with lice. Were it acceptable for men to behave as these men behave, we would be living, not in a world governed by order and the divinely inspired laws of the Crown, but in complete and utter anarchy. Were it the *will* of the *Almighty* that men dabble in strange and bizarre rituals, and adorn themselves with chintzy jewels, then these men would be upstanding citizens."

"Were it that you would *shut up* I might be able to avoid this throbbing headache," Jack said, and Teague, along with some of the officers, couldn't prevent himself from smirking.

"Silence!" the admiral commanded.

Jack straightened his back dramatically.

"Were all these things the reasonable lay of our land and sea, we would not be compelled to do what we are about to do. . . ."

The admiral turned to Teague. He held

out his hand, and an officer placed a rolled scroll in his open palm. Lawrence Norrington unrolled it and held it out ceremoniously.

"The pirate known as Teague—be it known that you have been charged, tried, and convicted for—"

"Wait, wait, wait just one moment," Jack said. "What's all this 'charged, tried, and convicted' business? Perhaps it's just me, but I don't recall anyone doing any charging or trying or convicting here."

The admiral shot Jack a scowling glance.

"Fine," the admiral said flatly. "The pirate known as Teague, you are charged with piracy," the admiral said.

"Very well, then," Jack said. "But what about the trying and convicting bit?"

"Gentlemen," the admiral shouted to his crew, "is this man, known as Teague, guilty of piracy?"

"Will there be a hanging if he is?" a strong voice rang out from the crowd.

"More likely a plank-walking, as I would rather not dirty my craft with pirate death."

"Almost as good, that. Guilty!" the voice shouted, and was joined quickly by the rest of the crew.

The admiral smiled smarmily, and Jack gulped.

"Now, if I may continue," the admiral said.

"The floor's all yours, mate," Jack said, motioning with a resigned acceptance.

"You have been tried and convicted for your willful commission of crimes against the Crown, said crimes being infinite in quantity and sinister in nature, the most egregious of those to be cited herewith: piracy, threatening members of the Royal Navy with their own weapons, threatening members of the Royal Navy with your own weapons, theft of a gaggle of geese from a wading pond outside of Boston, threatening members of the Royal Navy with said gaggle of geese, looting, arson, theft of a Royal Navy vessel, possessing an unlawful quantity of barley and hops, pillaging, cavorting with soothsayers, extortion, smuggling; and for these crimes you have been sentenced to be executed by hanging . . . or just generally killed somehow in the event that he who is officiating the execution does not care to sully his ship."

"I have a strange feeling you added that last part, about the ship-sullying and all . . ." Jack said.

"Keep silent!" the admiral barked. "The execution will take place at dawn. Oh, look, the sun seems to be creeping up over the horizon already. I suppose we needn't waste any more time, then."

"I must beg one more question first," Jack said snidely. "What is it that *I've* been charged, tried, and convicted of?"

"Guilt by association," the admiral said.

"Here, here!" a voice that sounded like Fitzwilliam's rang out.

"Men, secure the prisoners' hands and ready the plank," the admiral said.

A general milling about occurred on deck, as men tried to make way for the preparations.

Teague and Jack were brought to a clear spot on the deck where they were to be prepared for plank-walking. Teague looked up and smiled slightly. The man binding their hands so they could not struggle was none other than Mr. Gibbs.

"Sorry about all this," Gibbs whispered. "Why didn't you just flee when ye were off the ship?"

Teague glanced down at Jack, only slightly

irritated. Jack thought that Teague seemed to be enjoying this whole hullabaloo a great deal.

Mr. Gibbs tugged on their bonds. To Jack's surprise, they were tied tight.

"There is nothin' I can do. They'd suspect me if I gave ye any more slack. Pray for your souls, but with only your thumb and index finger pressed tightly together," Mr. Gibbs said mysteriously. And with that, he walked away.

Jack thought that this must truly be the end. There was no way out of this bind. After all he'd been through, after the mermaids and pirate kings, cursed swords and time-bending watches, it would end like this: walking a plank on an ordinary navy ship.

"Up you go," the admiral commanded. Jack and Teague ascended to the plank.

"Good riddance, Teague," the admiral said.

"And good riddance to you, as well," Teague responded with the air of a man who refused to die with anything but dignity.

"Walk," the admiral commanded flatly.

Teague began to walk the plank slowly, but evenly and steadily, without hesitation. Jack watched the pirate with a strange mix of consternation and regret. He was angry with the navy for what they were doing to Teague, but he was also bothered by the fact that now he and Teague would never be able to make amends. And most importantly, Jack would never find out what it really was he wanted to do with his life.

Teague finally reached the end of the plank and dropped off.

Jack had his eyes closed in anticipation of the telltale splash that would follow. His mind was racing, fixing on how long it would take a man with bound hands to drown out in the middle of the sea.

Then something happened . . . or didn't happen, rather. The splash Jack was waiting for never came. The admiral noticed this, too. He pushed away the boy, who had been clinging to his coat, and stormed onto the plank. He walked to the very edge, scanning the water below for traces of the pirate. Then he knelt down on the plank and peered beneath it. But before he could get a good look, something swung up from underneath the plank and hit the admiral.

It was Teague! He had somehow escaped his bonds and managed to grab the plank as he fell. Then, as the admiral inspected the water, Teague had hoisted himself up onto the plank behind him.

Quicker than Jack might have expected, the admiral had pulled his sword, Teague had stolen another from a soldier, and Norrington and Teague were dueling.

A chaotic ruckus erupted, and Jack felt relieved that he wouldn't have to walk the plank—for the moment at least.

"Psst!" Jack heard someone call from behind him. "There's a loose bit of rope between your forefinger and your thumb. Catch it and pull if you can, and you'll be freed."

Jack turned to see the wide, yellow smile of Mr. Gibbs, who winked at him. Jack quickly did as Mr. Gibbs had suggested, and the bonds came free. That was how Teague must have freed himself as well. Mr. Gibbs slyly slipped Jack's sword back to him. Armed, Jack pushed through the crowds upon the ship in search of one person.

"Not so quickly, worm," came a voice from behind him.

It was just the person he had been looking for—Fitzwilliam.

"I had no intention of attempting an escape," Jack said, realizing that it actually *had* crossed his mind before he settled on attacking Fitzwilliam.

Fitzwilliam began furiously striking away at Jack, who deflected the blows with his own sword. At first, the sleepy navy crew seemed strangely ambivalent as the two pairs of sword-fighting sailors danced about the ship. Then Jack realized that some of the officers had begun to fight among themselves. Jack thought this was strange. He hadn't much experience with the navy, but he knew them to be loyal to each other (or, at the very least, to the Crown) in a way that pirates were not.

Then, one of the navy sailors charged past Jack, who quickly recognized the sailor's crooked-toothed smile and tattoos as belonging to Renegade Robbie.

Jack smirked. While Teague had been on the *Barnacle*, the rest of his crew had gone back to the *Misty Lady*. But now, about a dozen of his crew had come back and infiltrated the navy ship. They were posing as members of the navy.

"Closer, ye dolts! Closer still!" Robbie yelled.

Jack could see that Robbie was calling out to the *Misty Lady*, which was being crewed by the handful of pirates that remained aboard the pirate ship. If the *Lady* could get close enough . . .

Just then, a rapid firing of cannons blasted from the port side of the ship.

Jack gasped, his eyes wide.

He had feared it before, but this time it had actually happened—the cannon fire, meant for the *Misty Lady*, had blown the *Barnacle* to bits! He watched as his boat split into multiple pieces, the mast burning, the deck collapsing on itself.

Jack felt a very large lump develop in his throat, and, to add insult to injury, at that moment, he was whacked with a serious blow to the shoulder. His distraction had allowed Fitzwilliam an advantage. Jack fell to the deck, while all around him the battle raged between the crews. Fitzwilliam smiled.

"I have waited, patiently, for quite some time to do this," Fitzwilliam said.

At that moment, a cry of anguish rang out, overpowering all other noise on the ship.

"Uncle!" Fitzwilliam shouted.

Jack looked confused for a moment, then realized that Fitzwilliam was talking about the admiral. Fitzwilliam must have been Norrington's nephew! It was Admiral Norrington who had shouted out in pain. He'd been hit hard by Teague.

Now Jack took advantage of Fitzwilliam's being distracted, delivering a blow that sent Fitzwilliam to the ground. The two boys were so tired from their battle that neither could find it in themselves to move from the deck.

From this vantage point, Jack noticed that the admiral's son had rushed to his father's side. Then, Jack noticed something else. The boy was backing away from Teague, terrified. But he was backing into a gap in the balustrade. If Jack didn't do something, the boy would fall into the sea.

Jack thought about this for a second. Like Fitzwilliam, the boy was related to the admiral. It was his *son*. But did that mean nothing good could come from him? He was just a boy, with a whole life ahead of him. He could find his own way. And wasn't it wrong to punish a child for the sins of his father? Isn't that what Jack was trying to prevent happening with respect to himself and Teague?

Jack decided to muster all the energy he could and run toward the boy in order to prevent him from backing off the ship.

But Jack's actions only scared the boy further. He was clearly terrified at the sight of a teenager who looked like, acted like, and cavorted with a pirate, running after him. The boy lost his footing and tumbled into the water.

Jack gasped.

"James!" the admiral shouted.

When no one made a move to help, Teague sighed. He delivered a strong blow to the admiral and leaped off the ship. Jack leaned over the railing and strained to see what was going on. Down below, Jack could see Teague swimming frantically, but there was no boy in sight. Then Jack saw Teague dip below the water, reemerging moments later with the boy, who appeared to be unconscious.

"There's a ladder right by ya!" Robbie shouted to Teague, who probably couldn't see the ship clearly, due to the rays of the rising sun behind it. Teague struggled to grip the ladder with his free hand, then ascended to the deck.

He quickly threw the boy down and began to resuscitate him.

Fitzwilliam hurried to the boy's side.

"James! If he is dead—" Fitzwilliam began.

"What?" Jack said, clearly having had enough of the back-and-forth. "What will you do, Fitzy? Mind you, none of us has put this child in danger. It was you and that unckie of yours over there. Bringing a kid like that into battle seems like a very wise decision now, does it not? Oh, don't bother answering that question. It's just like you people to put anyone around you at risk— even a child. And for what, Fitzy? For what?"

"You are a filthy pirate," Fitzwilliam said, his face so red it looked as though it would blister.

"Thank goodness for *that*, if this is the way you not-piratey people treat each other," Jack replied.

Just then the boy began to cough.

Teague nodded to his crew that the boy would be okay.

From across the deck, the admiral began to shout.

"Saved by a pirate, James. You stupid brat. You should have let yourself drown, boy. I would have rather that than a Norrington smeared with the taint of being indebted to a pirate!"

Jack thought this was just a little bit extreme. He shot a sneer in the admiral's general direction.

The navy crew was defeated. The cannon fire had ceased, and most of the men were laid out on the deck. Robbie yelled out that the *Misty Lady* was now alongside the navy ship, and Teague's men began to shoot grappling hooks from one boat to another to reboard.

"I trust you'll think twice before deciding to try your luck with me again," Teague said to the wounded admiral. "And if you do plan on making another advance, please do leave the children behind."

Then Teague motioned to Jack.

"Come on, Jackie."

Jack gave Fitzwilliam an angry, and perhaps even disappointed, look. Then he and Teague each grabbed a line and swung back onto the *Misty Lady*, leaving the defeated naval crew and their battered ship behind them.

CHAPTER TEN

Jack leaned over the bow of the *Misty Lady* and looked out to sea. The flotsam and jetsam that was once the *Barnacle* bobbed on the small swells in the distance. Teague's crew was readying the ship, hoping to gain some headway on the navy. True, the navy crew was so battered and bruised that it would take a while for them to get their ship up and running again, but Teague did not want to leave anything to chance.

Jack felt someone slide up beside him.

"You doing all right, then, Jackie?"

It was Teague.

"Well, if you put aside my having neither ship nor crew—not even a one of them, not even a slimy, backstabbing crew member who is really a spy in disguise—and being aboard the ship of someone you've recently run away from, then, yes, I gather I am perfectly fine. Dandy. Almost joyful even," Jack responded.

Teague sat down on a barrel beside Jack.

"I know it's not easy—all this figuring stuff out and growing and learning. And when I told you before that you weren't ready to be out at sea with me, I didn't mean you weren't *capable*. You just hadn't figured out what it meant to be a pirate. Maybe you still haven't. . . ."

"I've lost my crew and my ship. I've been betrayed and nearly killed. Isn't that what being a pirate is all about?" Jack said.

"Sometimes. But it's about a great many other things as well. I think you've already begun to figure some of those things out," Teague said, smiling knowingly.

Jack could not deny the sense that something about being here, aboard Teague's ship, felt right. There was something so freeing about it. And he always knew he felt at home out on the sea, so what better place to live out the rest of his days?

"Still, I was a captain before, and now—" Jack began.

"Jackie, let's be honest. That wasn't a ship, nor were you a captain," Teague replied.

Jack frowned, knowing that when all was said and done, Teague was right.

"But the *Barnacle* was *mine*. And my faithful crew—well perhaps the word 'faithful' is not *entirely* accurate—but I thought they were right fine sailors and a pleasure to sail with, except for that cat. And that aristo. A real, real pleasure. OK, maybe 'pleasure' is a bit of an overstatement."

"Jackie, boats, ships, crews—they will all come and go. You have yourself to look out for, and only yourself. That doesn't mean you don't do those things you know are right—specifically those things that are right for *you*."

"So, I gather now you're going to force me to come back with you," Jack said.

"Actually, I think you're learning quite a lot out here on your own. Do you want to come back?"

"No."

"Very well, then. We can leave you at our next port—Tortuga."

"Um, isn't there anywhere else you can leave me? Tortuga's where I got myself started in this whole mess."

Teague pondered Jack's question for a moment.

"Mr. Robbie, is there someplace we can drop Jackie off between here and Tortuga?"

"Well, there's Snowy Island,"* Robbie responded.

Jack quickly and frantically shook his head no.

"Not much for winter sports, then?" Robbie said.

"Not in the middle of the Caribbean, mate," Jack replied.

"And what about *Isla Hermosa*?" Teague asked.

"We can surely do that," Robbie answered, "There be a small village right outside the landing, you'll be able to get yerself back up and running again in no time, Jackie."

*Jack and his crew were there when snow began to fall on *Isla Fortuna*, back in Vol. 4, *The Sword of Cortés*.

Jack shrugged. It sounded no worse—or better, for that matter—than any of the other islands he'd found himself on since he stowed away.

"Great, then," Teague said, resting his hand on Jack's shoulder. "Oh, and you might want to take this. . . ." Teague slipped a ring off his right index finger.

Jack was taken aback and quickly tried to hide his own hands.

"It's okay, Jackie, I know you took one of my rings before you left town."

"But Tia Dalma said you were looking for me. Looking for it."*

"I had it confused with another ring. This one."

Jack's eyes grew wide.

"This was the one you wanted, wasn't it?

---

*The mystic of the Pantano River told Jack this in Vol. 4, *The Sword of Cortés*.

The one with that most unique property."

"What are you talking about? I know nothing about a ring with a most unique property," Jack said loudly for the sake of the crew.

"So, this is the one what can control people and make them do your bidding, eh?" Jack continued out of the corner of his mouth, so only Teague could hear.

"Yes, Jackie. But be warned, it's only worked twice, once seven years ago when I was fending off an angry washerwoman, and again a few hours ago when we were in the process of securing your boat from that backstabbing mate of yours."

Jack's eyes were wide, curious, and a little bit skeptical as he examined the ring. So this is how Teague got Fitzwilliam to obey his orders aboard the *Barnacle*. Jack figured that the ring's power must have eventually worn off, which would be how Fitzwilliam was able to betray Jack and Teague's location.

"So, how do I know when it is going to work and when it's, you know, not?"

Teague shrugged. "There doesn't seem to be a rhyme or reason to any of it. So in other words, it would be wise not to rely on it."

Jack slipped the ring on his finger. It immediately slipped off—Teague's fingers were much bigger than Jack's. Even the ring Jack had swiped from Teague before was bridged with floss. Jack stuck the ring on his thumb instead, where it remained secure.

"Well, thank you." Jack fidgeted with the first ring. "Err, you want this other one back?" Jack asked.

"Eventually. Not now."

Jack wondered what that was supposed to mean.

Then, as if he hadn't just been talking

to Jack, Teague turned around and began barking orders at his crew.

"Raise the mainsail, set a northeasterly course."

Jack looked out to sea and sighed. He felt as if he had come so far. And now—now, he was about to start over from scratch.

Epilogue

In the most beautiful town Jack had ever seen, set on the most beautiful island Jack had ever been on, the young sailor handed a man at the docks a handful of dinars that Teague had given him.

The man motioned to a small boat, bobbing at the edge of the dock. This boat was only large enough for one, maybe two, sailors. It had one sail and no name. It was equipped with two oars.

Jack climbed in and then pulled out his

compass. A woman who was beautiful, like everything else on the island, had told him that a great treasure was to be found a few leagues to the northwest, on an island with a very tall peak. Jack figured that if he rowed all night long and caught the wind just right, he could be there in less than a day. He didn't mind all the spare time he'd need to kill or that he'd be alone. After all, he had a lot to think about.

Did he want to live a pirate's life? Did he have a choice? Was it something that was just in his blood? Jack wasn't sure. But for the time being at least, he was planning on living life for the moment. And maybe that was his answer. Maybe that made him pirate enough already.

Don't miss the next volume in the continuing adventures of Jack Sparrow and the crew of the mighty Barnacle!

Poseidon's Peak

Jack is once again all alone, and he's on the hunt for a treasure that he's not even sure is real. But a mysterious band of pirates is also looking for the treasure, and if it does exist, will it be Jack or the pirates who find it first?